when my baby dreams of fairy tales

Adele Enersen

Balzer + Bray
An Imprint of HarperCollinsPublishers

Once upon a time, there was
a baby girl named Mila . . .

Far, far away in dreamland, where the lakes are blue as the sky,
and the white clouds look like fluffy sheep just waiting to be
counted, live Mila and her fairy-tale friends.

These are Mila's dreams.

When my baby dreams of being a princess . . .

she tosses and turns in her royal bed . . .

lets down her golden hair and

escapes to the garden . . .

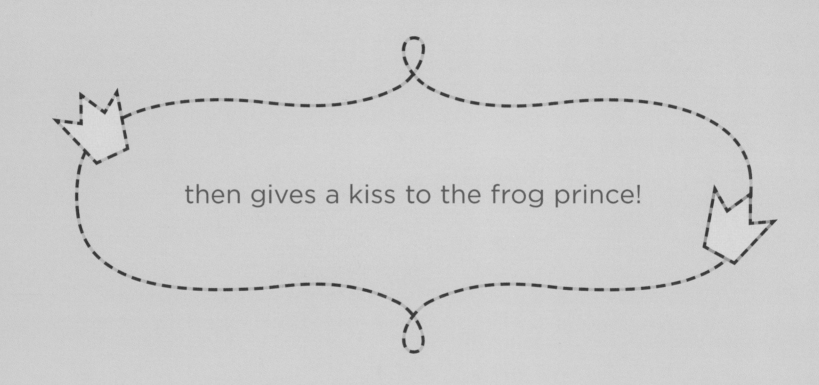

then gives a kiss to the frog prince!

Smack!

When my baby dreams of the big bad wolf . . .

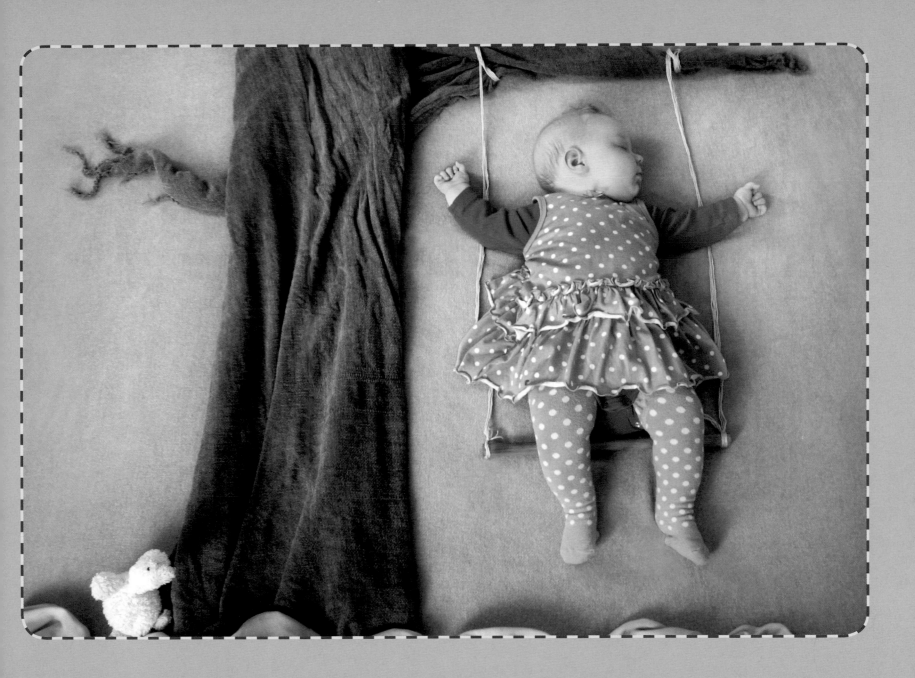

she hears whispers of something dangerous

hiding in the woods . . .

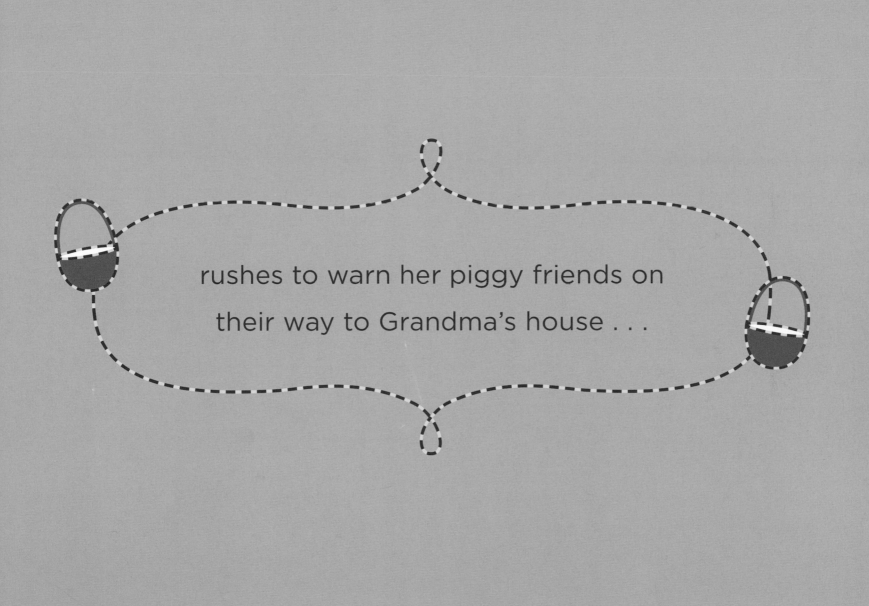

rushes to warn her piggy friends on their way to Grandma's house . . .

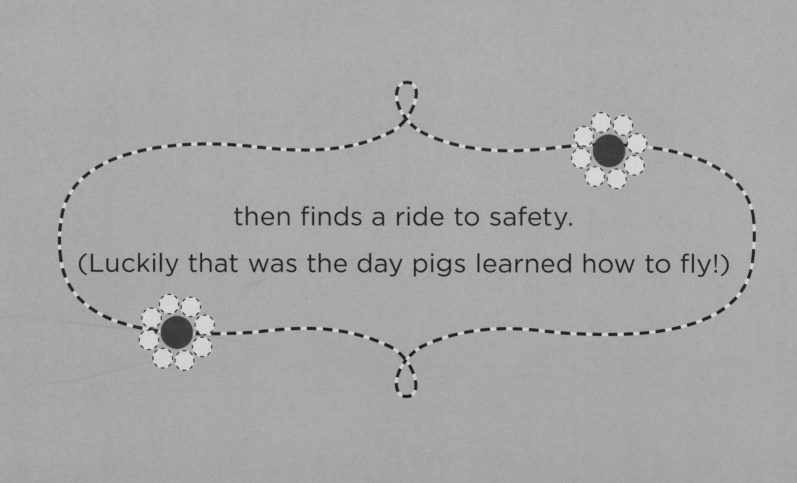

then finds a ride to safety.

(Luckily that was the day pigs learned how to fly!)

When my baby dreams of fairies . . .

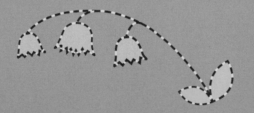

she jumps from flower to flower like Thumbelina . . .

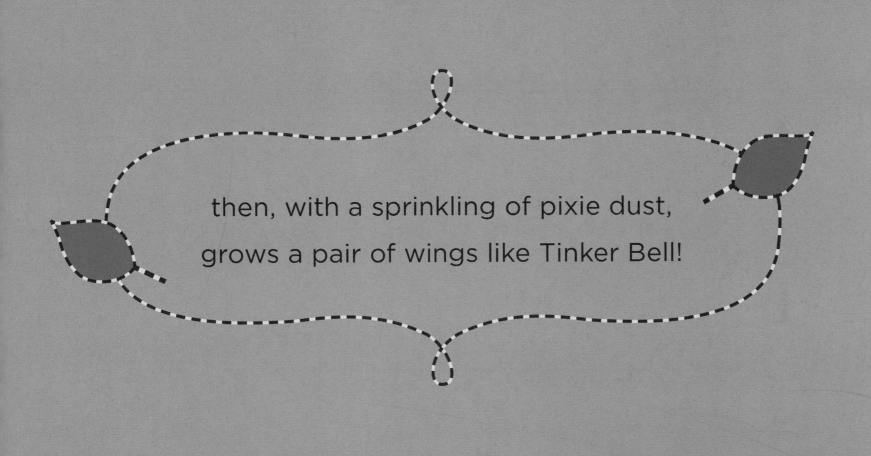

then, with a sprinkling of pixie dust,

grows a pair of wings like Tinker Bell!

When my baby dreams of the three bears . . .

she sets off on an adventure with the whole family . . .

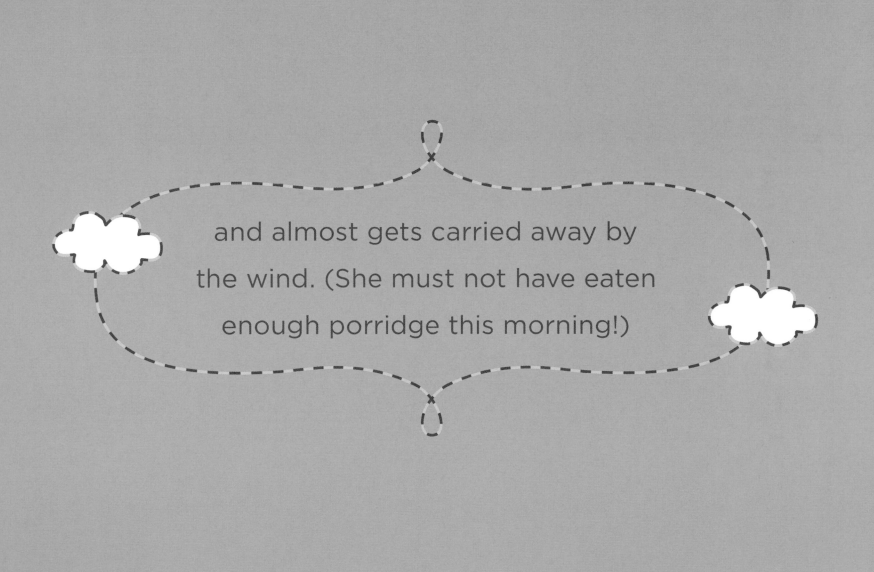

and almost gets carried away by the wind. (She must not have eaten enough porridge this morning!)

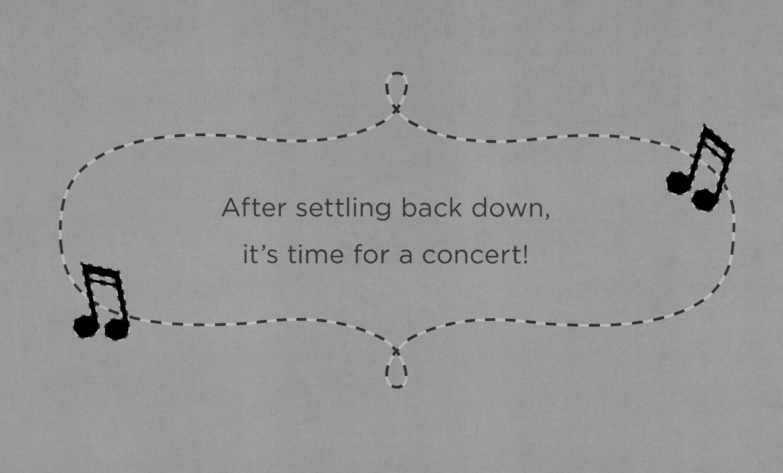

After settling back down,
it's time for a concert!

When my baby dreams of the ugly duckling . . .

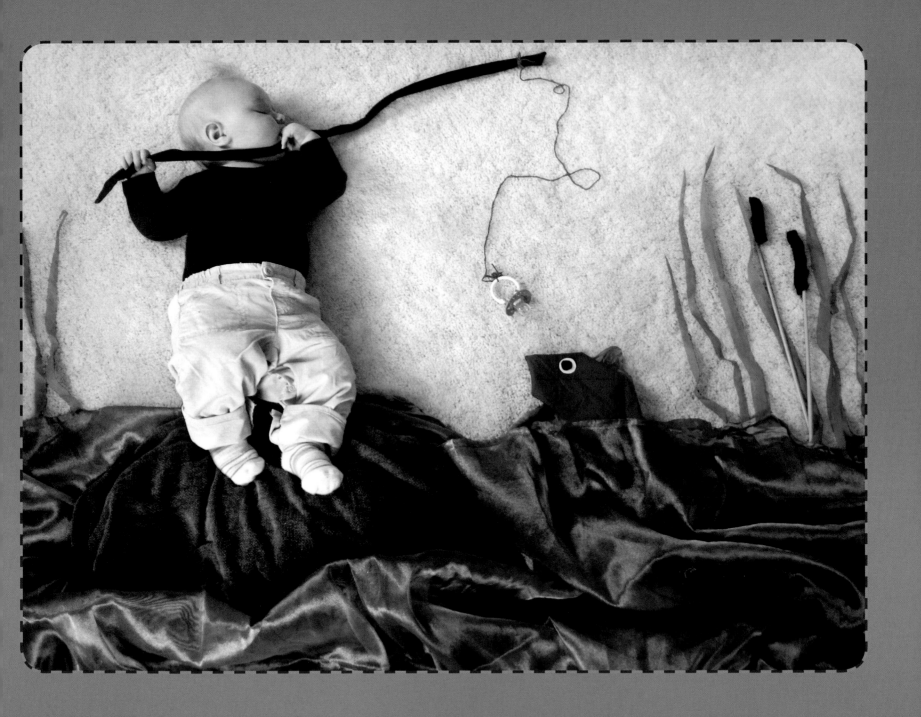

she fishes around, looking for her little feathered friend . . .

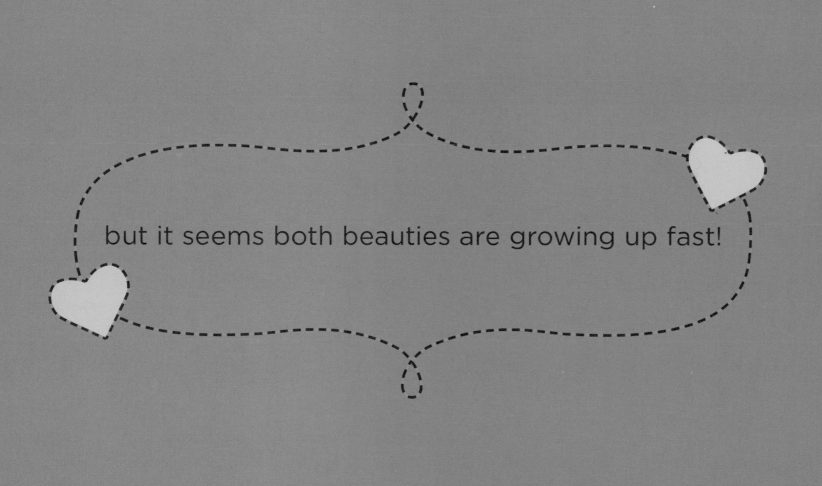

but it seems both beauties are growing up fast!

When my baby dreams of adventures far, far away . . .

she pops open her umbrella and soars into the sky,

all the way to outer space . . .

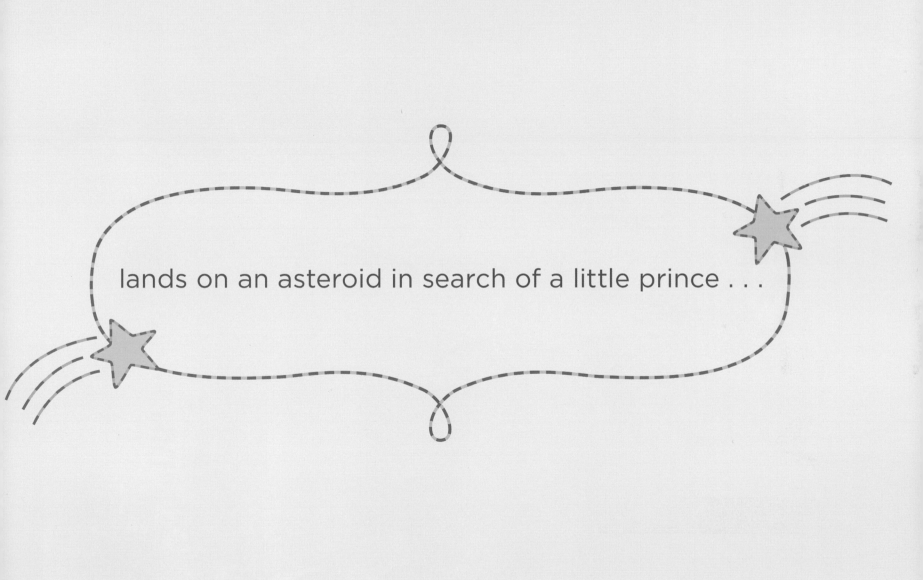

lands on an asteroid in search of a little prince . . .

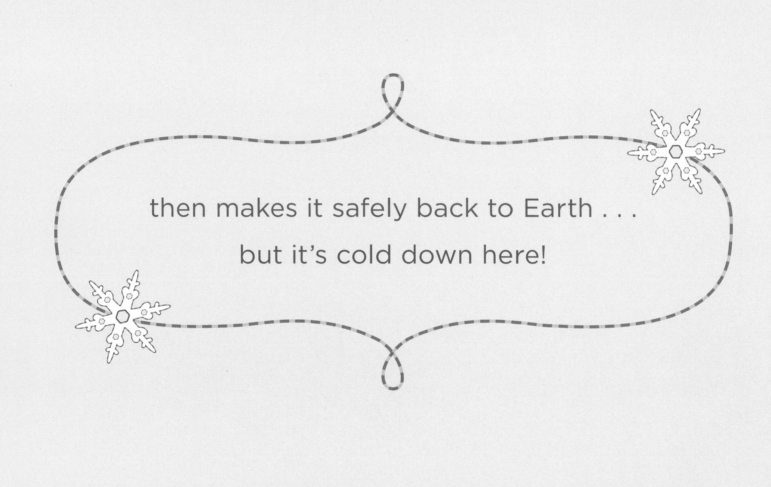

then makes it safely back to Earth . . .

but it's cold down here!

When my baby dreams of her fairy-tale friends . . .

she starts up a circus with her baby bear . . .

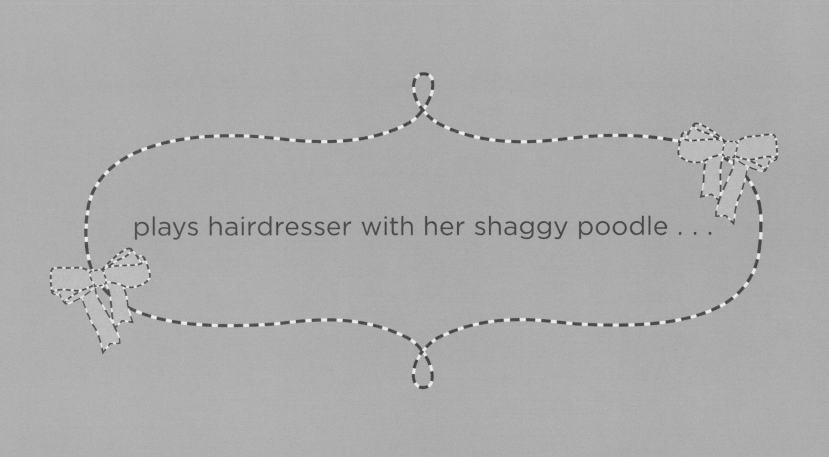

plays hairdresser with her shaggy poodle . . .

and since she can't find her friend

the bunny rabbit,

she'll dress up as one herself!

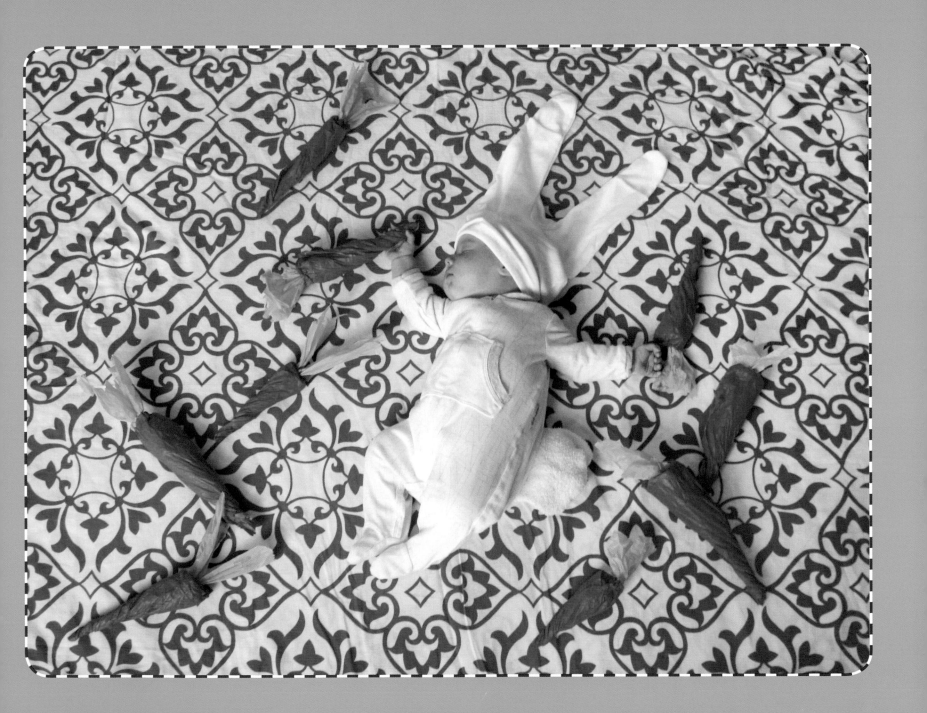

When my baby dreams of one thousand and one nights . . .

she flies above the seven seas on her magic carpet . . .

and with just a few wishes,

all her dreams come true!

When my baby finally wakes up . . .